CHESTER
the Chimpanzee

Written by
LES NUCKOLLS

Illustrated by
RACHEL SHARP

Sweetwater Books
an Imprint of Cedar Fort, Inc.
Springville, Utah

· ·

This book is dedicated to a fine
journalist, book author, and the best
traveling companion in the world—
my beautiful wife, Genevieve.

· ·

ISBN 13: 978-1-4621-1131-2

Published by Sweetwater Books, an imprint of Cedar Fort, Inc.
2373 W. 700 S., Springville, UT 84663
Distributed by Cedar Fort, Inc., www.cedarfort.com

LIBRARY OF CONGRESS CATALOGING-IN-PUBLICATION DATA

Nuckolls, Les, 1931- author.
Chester the chimpanzee / Les Nuckolls.
pages cm
Summary: The illustrated story of a pet chimp who was
raised from infancy by a young family living in Africa.
ISBN 978-1-4621-1131-2 (alk. paper)
[1. Chimpanzees--Fiction. 2. Americans--Africa--Fiction. 3. Africa--Fiction.] I. Title.

PZ7.N9633Che 2012
[E]--dc23

2012011274

Cover and page design by Brian Halley
Cover design © 2012 by Lyle Mortimer
Edited by Emily S. Chambers

Printed in China

10 9 8 7 6 5 4 3 2 1

Printed on acid-free paper

My family and I live in a cute little brick house.
Lots of people live in brick houses, but not like mine.
My brick house is smack-dab in the middle of Africa.

My name is Linda. We moved here from America
so my dad could help African teachers.

There's a little dirt road that runs by our house.
Lots of moms walk by, headed for the outdoor market.
It's very fun to see the babies tied on their backs.

"Hi, Linda," My friend Sundi greeted as she joined me.
Sundi and I are the same age. Her family lives right next door to mine.
They are a really fun African family.
We like to get together for cookouts and parties in the springtime,
right after the rainy season has ended.
Everything is beautiful and green this time of year.

We climbed into the swings that hung beneath the giant baobab tree.
My friend pointed down the road and said,
"Look, I see a car coming. Is it your dad?"

She was right. Dad pulled up and got out of the car.
He was dressed in his usual tan shorts and shirt.
However, he was different.
He was acting very strange.

"Come here, girls—I want to show you something!" he shouted.
Excited, we ran toward him. There was something in his arms.
He opened the small blanket he held. "What do you think?" he asked.

Sundi and I gasped. There was a small animal in his arms.
It was about the size of one of my large dolls.
It was wearing a diaper that covered part of its hairy body.
And, as if that wasn't enough, it was sucking on a baby bottle.
All I could say was, "Wow! What is it?"

"It's a baby chimpanzee. He's about eight weeks old.
The kids found him wandering around school. He must be lost."

"Can we keep him?" I asked my dad.

"I think we can. You'll have to take very good care of him though."

I looked at Sundi and said, "We will!"
Sundi was nodding and smiling from ear to ear.

That afternoon, we gave our new baby a bath.
"Linda, what should we name this little guy?" Sundi asked.

We thought up lots of ideas. Then, at the same time, we both said "Chester!"
We loved the name. We both agreed he looked like a perfect Chester.

In the coming weeks, our baby grew like a weed. He also seemed to be gaining
weight after every meal. Soon, he stopped crawling and ran everywhere.
Our little chimp loved his new home.

It wasn't long before Chester was eating with my family at the dinner table.
He learned to use a spoon and to drink from a small, plastic cup.
His favorite meal was bananas.

Chester was always careful. He tried not to make a mess.
If he did spill, he would start to cry, and I would clean it up.
But he did like a good food fight now and then . . .

When my mom and dad left the table, he sometimes acted silly.
He would throw pieces of bread at me. If I threw them back,
he would scream with laughter. He thought it was so much fun!

Chester grew bigger and bigger each day.
He loved to be pushed on the swings.
Afterward, he would scramble up the swings
into the huge baobab tree growing above us.

High up in the tree, he jumped fast from branch to branch.
Then he would hang by his knees upside down and wave at us below.
There was always a giant smile on his face.
He was a born circus performer.
We liked to call him "Chester the Clown!"

After his show, he would climb down.
We always knew what he wanted next if he pointed at the baby carriage.
Chester would climb inside, get comfortable,
and we would cover him with his blanket.
Then, we would sing to him while we pushed him around the yard.

One day, Chester and I had played until we were covered in dirt. We both needed a bath.
He loved hopping in the tub and often begged for a bubble bath.

With the warm water running, I poured in the bath soap.
As huge bubbles popped up everywhere, Chester screamed with delight.
Soon, all you could see was my head and Chester's grinning face above the foam.

My little hairy friend scrubbed himself from head to toe.
When he knew he had done a good job, it was time to play.

Without warning, he slapped his hand in the water,
and a big ball of bubbles hit me square in the face.
"Okay! If that's what you want!" I yelled.
Kicking my feet, a soapy wave splashed right over his head.

The bubble bath battle was on! I threw handfuls of bubbles at him with rapid fire!
He returned my attack by launching a washcloth at my head.
We were having the time of our lives.

When we'd had enough, we climbed out and mopped up the wet floor.

Chester thought of himself as a member of our family, and he was.
He thought Sundi and I were his sisters, even though he treated us more like mothers.
He loved us, and we loved him.

Chester was very smart, and he learned to play all of our games.
His favorite game was "Dress Up."
There was a big box in my closet.
It was full of all kinds of old clothes and shoes.
Sometimes Sundi and I dressed up in ladies' dresses and high-heeled shoes.
Looking fancy, we paraded around the house.

Once, after Sundi and I were dressed up, we found Chester going through the box.
He was wearing a long dress, high-heeled shoes, and a big flowery hat!
His round, hairy face looked funny under his bonnet.
When he stood in front of the mirror, he smiled at his reflection.
He thought he looked so beautiful.
Sundi and I laughed and laughed.

One summer morning the three of us dressed up like African women.
We wrapped ourselves in long pieces of pretty cloth.
They call them "Wrappers."

We put oranges in small baskets and then balanced them on our heads.
Walking carefully not to spill the fruit,
we made our way out to the little dirt road.

The African mothers smiled happily when they saw how we were dressed.
They gave us a penny for each of our oranges.
When they bought one from Chester,
he gave them a big hug!

Another day, Sundi and I were drawing pictures in my living room.
We heard the patter of little feet as Chester entered the room.
From the look on his face, we could tell he was bored.

He walked to the window and pointed out at the road,
and we knew at once what he wanted to do.

We ran in my room and put on dresses. When we got outside,
we grabbed the baby carriage and Chester squeezed inside.
We covered him with a little blanket and pushed the carriage out on the road.
Several moms carrying babies were near us.

"Can we look at the baby?" The ladies asked.
"Of course!" I said.

We moved away as all the women gathered round and peeked into the carriage.

At that exact moment, Chester ripped off the blanket.
He sat up with a huge grin on his hairy face.
Then he reached out toward them with his long arms.

"Help!" the women screamed. They had hoped to see a little baby.
Instead, they saw a hairy monster that was trying to grab them!
They all ran away screaming. Sundi and I just covered our mouths and laughed.

One time we had a tea party in my front yard.
There were flowers on the table and everything was just perfect.
My mom had made special chocolate cookies for us.

"Isn't this a lovely day for a tea party? There's not a cloud in the sky!" Sundi said.
I agreed as I took another bite of my delicious cookie.

Just then, I thought I heard water running.
It was like someone had turned on the garden hose.
"Sundi, do you hear water?"

Suddenly, Chester leaped out from around the house with the garden hose in his hands.
The water was running fast and hard. We both screamed, "Chester, NO!"

Our hairy attacker roared with laughter.
He aimed the stream of water at our tea table and
drenched both of us to the skin.

We were soaked and our cookies were ruined.
Chester continued to cackle with joy.
Then, dropping the hose, he ran off to the backyard.
His sneak attack was a complete success.

Halloween came. I had lots of fun at school where I dressed up like a ghost.
I wore a large, white pillowcase over my head.
My dad cut out two holes for eyes so I could see.
All of the other kids wore costumes too.

That evening, I was sitting at the dinner table with my mom and dad.
We were talking about my fun day at school.
Suddenly, there was a loud banging noise against the kitchen window!
It frightened us all!

We turned and stared out the window. It was almost dark outside.
Still, we could see a large, white ghost peering at us through the glass.
It made weird, spooky sounds that really scared me!

Then, even in the darkness we could see long hairy arms.
Hidden under the pillowcase we saw a furry face.
The hairy ghost made one last shriek as he ran off giggling to the backyard.
Chester had struck again!

One day I came down sick with the flu.
"No visitors for you!" my mom told me.

When Mom was busy elsewhere in the house, Chester would sneak into my bedroom.
He would sit on a little stool next to my bed and look at me with a sad face.

The second day, Mom said I had a fever. Then she left my room to do chores.
I lay there with my eyes closed. I was so hot and miserable.

Suddenly, something cold and wonderful touched my forehead!
I didn't know what it was, but I wanted it to stay!
Opening my eyes, I looked up to see Chester standing over my bed.
In his hand, he held a cool washcloth that he had soaked in cold water.
Holding it gently on my forehead, he made comforting little purring sounds to me.

A few minutes later we heard Mom's footsteps.
Chester dashed out the door just in time.
I smiled to myself. Chester was my best friend.

Christmastime finally came and we decorated a large tree.
It was fun watching Chester hang colorful balls on the green limbs.

My father had an old Santa Claus costume,
and he had worn it to my class that day for our Christmas party.
The kids loved him.
Later, he returned the costume to his bedroom closet.

All day, Mom baked and baked.
She made enough cookies to last us to Valentine's day!

The next morning was Christmas.
I was still sleeping when Dad burst into my room.
"Wake up!" he yelled. I jumped up, still in my pajamas.
"Come and see!" he said.

We ran to the front window.
Dad pointed out at the little dirt road.
There was a large group of African children gathered there.
They looked so happy and excited
because someone was passing out cookies to them.

Then I spotted him. Santa was in the middle of the kids.
He wore a red hat with a white ball hanging from it.
On his face he had a white cotton beard.
His red coat and pants finished off his costume.
And, in his arms he held a large bag filled with cookies!

Santa was handing each of the children a wonderful treat.
And that's when I saw them.
Santa had hairy hands sticking out of his coat sleeves!

"Dad, Santa is Chester! He's giving those kids Mom's Christmas cookies!"
The Santa outfit was far too big for him, but somehow Chester made it work.
"How could he know how to do that?" I asked my father.

"I have no idea," he replied. "But doesn't he make a perfect Santa?
Maybe he knew because he was raised in a loving family."

I reached over and gave my dad a great big hug.

"Thanks for bringing Chester home that day, Dad.
He's the best friend a girl could ever ask for."

THE END

WHATEVER HAPPENED TO CHESTER?

After raising Chester for two years, we had to return to California.
I was very sad when I gave my best friend to our neighbors next door.

However, Chester knew Sundi and her family well, and he loved them.
I knew he would be well cared for.

Chester is now a full-grown male chimpanzee.
He is healthy and as full of fun and mischief as ever.

A happy and healthy chimp can live to be fifty years old or older.
There is no doubt Chester will do just that.

I still miss him, but I know that he is safe.

I will always remember the many adventures I shared with Chester.

ABOUT THE AUTHOR

LES NUCKOLLS and his wife, Genny, are both native Californians with a love for travel and writing. Over the years they have had regular columns in several newspapers and more recently coauthored the books *Growing Up in Africa* and *A Boy Named Walter*.

During a long career as an educator, Les taught at an African college as a Presidential Fulbright Scholar and later served as a consultant to the government of Nigeria and the US Peace Corps. During his years as a department head at UCLA, he developed programs in Africa and Latin America.

Les was living and working in Africa when he met a furry little baby he named "Chester the Chimpanzee."

RESIDENCE: Roseville, California

ABOUT THE ILLUSTRATOR

RACHEL SHARP grew up and attended public schools in the small town of Weiser, Idaho. She is currently working with fourth and fifth graders as a teacher's aide. She also teaches mini art lessons to students in an after-school program.

Since completing high school, Rachel has improved her artistic skills through independent study and practice. Her first break into the world of illustrating books came from a local author, Donna Peterson, who admired her work and asked her to illustrate *The Misadventures of Phillip Isaac Penn*. Rachel just finished illustrating the sequel to that book, *PIP Goes to Camp*. She also Illustrated the cover for *Benotripia: The Rescue*.

RESIDENCE: Weiser, Idaho